Alana's Sweet Baby

An MDLG and ABDL lesbian romance about a baby girl who didn't know just how into age play she was until her Mommy's seductive introduction.

By Tina Moore

Table of Contents

Chapter 1

"Yes, baby, that's it," Alana moaned as the young French girl she had picked up at a less than savory back street fingered herself in front of Alana's greedy eyes. The girl, who Alana hadn't bothered learning the name of, reached for her cigarette that was burning out in the ashtray. Pouting as her hand was slapped away aggressively by Alana, who refocused her camera lens. The night had been long with Alana having her fill with the boney girl before making her touch herself, just the way Alana liked.

"Don't you dare fucking stop," she commanded, grabbing the girl's loosely curled auburn hair and kissing her passionately before pushing her head back down and watching her through her lens. The girl writhed on the bed of the cheap motel, rented by Alana for the sole purpose of capturing her youthful vulnerability.

"Cum for Mommy," Alana instructed, throwing a couple of hundred dollar bills onto the girl's face.

"You're just a sweet little fuck toy aren't you baby girl," Alana said, narrowing her eyes as the girl began to arch her back and close her eyes. Alana slapped her tits, making her open her eyes again suddenly and nod her head, her sweet eyes looking for everything except what Alana was willing to give her. Alana moved around the head of the bed and took her panties off, sitting on the girl's face and riding her mouth as she photographed her pussy and thighs. The girl gasped, making Alana laugh, and she lifted off her slightly, allowing the girl to pant for air, her young ribs heaving and protruding under her soft skin as Alana tenderly ran her fingers over them.

"Such a pretty little thing," Alana said, getting off the girl's face and kissing her mouth clean before untying her ankles and watching as the girl half cowered in the corner of the bed, unsure of what Alana wanted with her next.

"Come here," Alana said, rolling her eyes and opening her arms to the girl who gladly crawled to her and snuggled into Alana's older body, getting enveloped by her large breasts.

"Suck," Alana said, rubbing her swollen nipple over the top of the girl's lips, smiling as she parted them instinctively and began suckling on the older woman. Alana lit a cigarette and inhaled deeply before she took her camera and started clicking again, making the girl look up at her, her wide eyes asking to be taken, her mouth full like the slut that she was.

Alana was 33 before she became an internet success. Before then, she had just been another photographer working a crappy day job while she tried to sell her art online. Photography was more than just art for Alana. It was a way to escape the disappointing world around her, where people shielded their true and most pure desires behind stressful jobs and mundane lifestyles. For Alana, the more well-known her art became, the easier it was for her to slip away from that kind of existence and into her world. A world where she could take women with the ferocity, she craved to express and without the guilt of enjoying a new woman when and where she wanted. With a steady stream of high paying clients funding her lifestyle, Alana was not surprised when an email came that offered her access to a successful young entrepreneur. A girl called Rosie. Rosie portrayed everything Alana hated about the world, but Alana had agreed to photograph Rosie after Rosie's people had said they would pay her to stay in one of the nicest hotels on the Upper East Side. Rosie was beautifully fake, with everything about her either altered or pretend. She was the definition of a millennial and had become famous for doing nothing but marketing herself and her lifestyle with a genius only a narcissist could pull off. Companies now gave her their product to get a mention on her accounts, and Alana was to capture Rosie in a series of photos that were to be auctioned off at a charity event. When Rosie's people had asked her how long it would take Alana to do the series, she had lied and said three weeks. She knew it would take her less than two, but she wasn't about to let this little attention-seeking bitch keep her from enjoying the city. Alana planned to finish the series as fast as she could so that she could spend the rest of her time finding a new muse. That thought excited her. The things she wanted to do to a sweet, young, dependent girl made her cunt drip with anticipation.

"Oh my god, look at how fantastic this is, this is lit!" Rosie squealed, looking at Alana's page.

"It's like, sexy but serious," Rosie added. Alana just bit her tongue and tried to stay calm as she wondered what it would take to get Rosie to stop talking. She looked at Rosie with her perky tits and whitened teeth and smirked as she imagined smudging her indigo lipstick as she backhanded her across the face making her sparkling eyes water. She also found herself wondering what Rosie's pussy looked like if everything else she could see had been augmented. *I bet it's perfect;* she thought slowly closing the lid of her computer. Rosie pouted and looked at her with puppy dog eyes.

"If you want me to photograph you like that," Alana said, nodding to her computer, "You'll have to take your clothes off," Alana continued. Rosie had selected a series of nude photos, and Alana smiled when Rosie nodded her head as though she had just been asked if she wanted syrup on her waffles. *Wow, it's nothing to her,* Alana thought watching Rosie. Today she was only going to do a few test shots to get a feel for the style Rosie wanted and sat back as Rosie began to take her clothes off in front of her. Rosie smiled at Alana as she pulled off her low cut singlet and folded it neatly, placing it down on the coffee table. She kicked off her heels and left them on the floor as she stood up and unbuttoned the top of her skirt.

"Does this mean I'm your muse?" Rosie said softly, for the first-time showing Alana a more vulnerable side. Rosie unzipped her skirt before tripping on her heels, stumbling backward. Alana involuntarily jumped to her feet and grabbed Rosie, pulling her body to hers and holding it there firmly with her hand grabbing Rosie's ass and the other snaking up her back holding the back of her head. What Alana didn't know was that this was the safest Rosie had ever felt, being held in the arms of the older, curvier woman.

"No, this means that I'm going to photograph all of this," Alana said almost lovingly, matching the softness in Rosie's voice before grabbing the hem of the skirt and pulling it off in one quick motion. Rosie gasped, feeling exposed for the first time in her 22 years and suddenly became shy, standing only in her underwear in front of Alana. Letting her go, Alana smiled as the overconfident ball of energy turn into a shy, little girl in front of her eyes.

"You have to keep going, sweetheart, you're not done yet," Alana said, finding her seat again and crossing her arms over her chest, enjoying the young girl's discomfort. Rosie just nodded as she slowly unclipped her black and red lace bra and placed it on top of her singlet, followed by her panties. Alana stood and took Rosie's hand as she passed, walking the naked girl through her own house and up to her bedroom.

"This is where you said you wanted it to be done, yes?" Alana said to a silently nodding Rosie.

"Well?" Alana said, raising her eyebrow and speaking more commandingly to Rosie, wanting more than just a nod. Alana looked at Rosie like she might devour her with her eyes, making Rosie swallow hard.

"Yes," Rosie replied, slightly pulling away from Alana and looking down to the ground.

"Uh-huh sweetie, you're going to have to get used to me seeing you like this, or it'll be a long three weeks for you. Come on, lay down for me," Alana said, gently laying Rosie down in the position she wanted her in. Going to her wardrobe, Alana smiled as she traced over the girl's lingerie, stopping when she saw a red lace panty and bra set. Coming back, swinging the garments around on her finger, Alana threw them at Rosie.

"Put that on, I want to see something," Alana instructed as Rosie began to obey. Alana watched as Rosie dressed, her slender fingers adjusting the panties and pausing, unsure of what Alana wanted from her now. Alana pressed on Rosie's shoulders, making her lay back down as she got to work.

"There," Alana said in satisfaction as she placed a pillow under Rosie. She had positioned her so that she was on her tummy, leaning more to one side. She had taken red lipstick that was on Rosie's sideboard and carefully painted her lips, enjoying how Rosie blushed when Alana had winked at her. Alana had taken out Rosie's long brown hair and let it fall to its own accord and tilted her head up, making her mouth look ready to be fucked. Alana ran her hands over Rosie's slender body, taking in her curves.

"Stay still for me sweetie, I need you to hold that for a little while longer," Alana said seeing

Rosie shift uncomfortably. Alana walked over to the bed and placed additional pillows around Rosie's hips, enjoying the subtle warmth that came from her thighs to help support her. Alana felt the all too familiar stirring deep within her as Rosie pressed her head into Alana's palm when she cupped her face.

"Good girl," Alana said lovingly, looking into Rosie's eyes and stroking her cheek with her thumb, hating that she was getting wet with the control and proximity she had with the untouchable girl.

Chapter 2

Alana had two other photo sessions with Rosie and had enjoyed touching Rosie more and more with each shoot. Once Alana had made her sit straddling a pillow so that she could reach between Rosie's thighs and reposition it. Alana had taken the time to stroke Rosie's slit gently and felt her clit tingle, watching as Rosie looked away nervously, her face burning red but the wetness being easily felt on Alana's fingertips. Today, she had laid her on her back and draped a fur blanket over the top of her, having Rosie wrap her arms around her neck as Alana skillfully unhooked her bra. Today Rosie was too shy to strip in front of Alana, and she had begged to be covered. Alana had agreed, helping Rosie take off her bra and panties before bothering to ask if it was alright to do so, happy when Rosie moved so obediently for her. Alana felt herself become more and more drawn to Rosie, her long brown hair always sitting so perfectly, and her come fuck me eyes always staring at Alana made her wet with desire.

"Come here, sweetheart, I want to show you what I've done," Alana said, smiling at Rosie, who grabbed a robe and quickly tied it in place. She didn't have her usual arrogance today, and Alana could almost swear she saw Rosie fight back the tears on more than one occasion. Rosie walked over to where Alana was sitting and placed the series of photos in front of her, who looked at them carefully. She liked how Alana had captured her, but she knew they wouldn't sell. Alana had made her look innocent, and that wasn't what people wanted. They wanted the party girl, the one who dominated and teased the crowds. Rosie looked at her reflection in the photos and bit her bottom lip.

"They are beautiful, but they aren't going to work," she quietly said, making Alana frown.

"You said you wanted yourself captured in them. I did that," Alana questioned, confused as to why Rosie didn't like them. Rosie took Alana's hand, making Alana flinch slightly and look at Rosie in her eyes.

"You're the only person who has looked at me like that and been able to see this, and I wish you wouldn't Alana," Rosie said, tilting her head to the photos on Alana's screen, making Alana smirk at the compliment.

"It's not my fault I see past all of this," Alana said, gesturing to Rosie's body and then looking around the grand room they were sitting in. Rosie looked up and let her eyes roam around the room. The marble floors and gold fixtures reflected the light from the chandelier; the artwork on the walls did nothing to make the room cozier.

"I need the photos to be more like this," Rosie said, suddenly switching back to her soulless princess manner. She took out her phone and showed Alana a photo of her wearing a dress, sitting on a motorbike, and looking seductively down a camera lens. Alana looked at the photo and looked back at Rosie, who had taken her hand away.

"You want me to turn you into a little slut?" Alana asked, annoyed that Rosie had put her wall back up. Rosie laughed and got up, starting to walk towards the door.

"What? That's what you thought you'd be doing when you first got here, wasn't it?" Rosie said, leaving the room. Alana watched her as she left and turned back to look at the photo on Rosie's phone. *If she wants to be a slut, I'll make her a fucking slut*, Alana thought putting her laptop with the images of a doe-eyed Rosie in her satchel.

Alana only needed one shoot to get the images Rosie craved and even then had rushed it, annoyed that Rosie was determined to have the world believe something that wasn't true.

"We're done?" Rosie said, put out that the shoot was so fast, it had been less than an hour when Alana began putting her camera equipment away and tried to hide the smile that crept across her face.

"Yeah, baby girl, we are," she replied, looking up at Rosie and brushing her hair out of her eyes. Alana's loose ponytail allowed her wispy hair to fall out around her face, framing it elegantly. Alana came to sit on the bed she had left Rosie on and bit her bottom lip as she ran her fingers through Rosie's hair, taking a gamble on the young woman in front of her.

"I mean, I could stay?" Alana asked, imagining how sweet Rosie would look like as her baby. The onesies she could put her in would, Alana guessed, take her less than an hour to get comfortable in. Rosie lifted her head and crawled her way into Alana's lap, much to the excitement of the older woman.

"You don't know what you're getting yourself into, sweetheart," Alana half laughed as she continued to feel Rosie's naked body against hers. Alana took the blanket that she had used to cover Rosie for the shoot and wrapped it around her as she felt Rosie's skin turn cold.

"Such a sweet baby. If I had known you

were so sweet, I would have tried to meet you earlier," Alana said, knowing that she had to give the girl back but wishing she could take her home and keep her. Alana looked into Rosie's eyes and saw the baby trying to stay grown up, and Alana knew that their embraced needed to end before Rosie's heart attached itself to her the way only a little does.

"Come on, time to get dressed, you've got a lot of things to do today, sweet baby," Alana said gently pushing Rosie from her arms and going back to packing up her equipment as Rosie stood and looked blankly at Alana before leaving the room to get dressed.

Alana spent the next few days editing the photos and was in the middle of editing them when her phone rang. She ignored it, letting it ring out, hoping to finish detailing the motorbike Rosie was sitting on before the end of the day, stopping angrily when her phone rang twice. She didn't bother to see who was on the other side before she answered.

"What?!" Alana yelled down the phone, angry to be ripped out of her concentration. Her rage soon turned to concern when she heard Rosie crying on the other end.

"I'm sorry, I just didn't know how else to call," Rosie said, making Alana soften instantly.

"Hey, what's happened?" She asked, getting up from her computer and going out to the balcony. Alana lit a cigarette and blew smoke into the night air. She hadn't realized it was so late until this moment and had to crane her ears to hear Rosie as a police siren rang down the street.

"There was this meet and greet I had to go to, and I was meeting people and went backstage with one of the interviewers, and he got grabby. He told me that it didn't matter what I said, that no one would believe me anyway and that he could get me more coverage if I didn't refuse him," Rosie said, crying into the phone. Alana frowned, she knew she was going to be drawn into Rosie's world, she knew that having a connection to her would mean she wouldn't be able to hide from the media like she had been enjoying, but she also knew that she couldn't deny the feelings she had for the girl.

"Can you come to my hotel? What did you do about the guy?" Alana asked, walking back inside and looking at the beautiful slut she had on her screen and shook her head.

"Yeah I can come, I know where you are. I told him to get fucked, but like still, I let him do some stuff before I told him that and like, just yuck," Rosie said, making Alana smiled at her choice of words.

"Well, I'll be waiting for you. Have you eaten?" Alana said, hoping she wouldn't scare Rosie off.

"It's Wednesday, I don't eat on Wednesdays," Rosie said bluntly.

"Oh right, sorry, I forgot," Alana said as she began to order a pizza online. Rosie had told her that BBQ chicken with pineapple was her favorite pizza during one of their photoshoots.

"It's OK. See you soon; I'm getting in a car now," Rosie said before quickly hanging up.

Half an hour later, Alana heard a knock on her hotel door and knew it would either be her pizza or Rosie, laughing when it was both.

"I've got your order, Miss," Rosie said, smiling softly at Alana. Alana raised an eyebrow at Rosie, who just laughed and pushed past her.

"Have you got beer? It's past midnight so technically not Wednesday anymore," Rosie said, causing Alana to roll her eyes as she looked in the fridge, pulling out a six-pack.

"Yum. Did you order this for me?" Rosie asked, closing her eyes and chewing slowly.

"Maybe," Alana said, opening two beers with her lighter and passing Rosie one.

"Thanks for this, I know you've got work to do. I just wanted to be somewhere; I don't know," Rosie said, turning to look at the photos Alana was in the process of completing.

"Safe?" Alana suggested draping a blanket

over Rosie's shoulders. It was the middle of winter, and Rosie only had a light jacket on, thigh-high black suede boots and a short dress. In any other apartment that would have been more than enough, but Alana had turned the heating off, enjoying the cold air on her skin and being able to rug up indoors. Rosie pulled the blanket around her body and shivered as she nodded, looking at Alana with those same doe eyes that Alana had captured only days ago.

"Well, you're safe now, baby," Alana said, taking a slice of pizza and taking off the pineapple, putting it on Rosie's slice. Rosie looked up at Alana, and Alana knew what was coming next.

"You don't have to do anything sweetie, I'm not like that guy," Alana said, stopping Rosie as she went to kiss her.

"I know you're not. But I've wanted to kiss you since I first saw you. Please?" Rosie said, placing her hand on Alana's thigh. Alana shifted uncomfortably.

"If you're going to kiss me, you'll have to do

it like this," Alana said, picking Rosie up swiftly and placing her on her lap, wrapping her arms around her and tilting her back slightly so that Rosie was being cradled in Alana's arms. She looked down at Rosie and rolled her body over slightly so that Rosie was pressed into Alana's chest and breathed with relief when she felt Rosie relax in her arms.

"Shh little one, you're safe now," Alana said as she felt Rosie start to cry. Rosie brought her arms up to her chest and gently pushed against Alana, trying to get up, but Alana just gripped her tighter.

"Ugh ugh don't push Mommy away," Alana said soothingly, as she looked down into Rosie's eyes tenderly, watching a tear escape as Rosie gave in and melted into the embrace resting her head against Alana's generous breasts in surrender, sucking her thumb as she was rocked.

"This could easily be seen as sexual harassment Alana. You said you weren't like that guy," Rosie said with no real intention of ever calling her out on it.

"Do you feel harassed? Am I asking you do anything as he did? Or do you feel like you enjoy being cared for the way you need it? The way you dream of being taken cared of? Being in the arms of a Mommy who can see that you're just a little girl who needs to be looked after," Sabine replied knowingly, a smug smile spreading across her face as she unbuttoned her blouse, enjoying Rosie's fingertips tracing over the edge of her bra.

"You're lucky you read me well," Rosie whispered, wanting to stop the flood of emotions rushing her body as Alana pulled the top of her bra down and watched as Rosie began nursing instinctively.

"Ha, you're the easiest read sweet thing. Come on, tell Mommy what happened, not tonight, but before, from the beginning," Alana said gently, running her fingers through Rosie's hair and holding it back, making her look up at her.

"I wouldn't know where to start, Mommy," Rosie replied, shaking her head, letting her hair fall out of Alana's fingers. She dried her tears, got up, and rested against a wall. Alana stayed sitting on the sofa watching the girl she wanted so badly to own, struggle with her demons, and exhaled in frustration.

"I've got you, nothing bad is going to happen to you now, little one," Alana said as Rosie walked back to her and lay back down, getting gently rocked in Alana's loving arms.

Chapter 3

Alana held Rosie through the night, feeding her pizza and watching as she got drunk in her arms, not wanting to be let go. As the night reached midnight, Alana carefully placed Rosie down in her bed and tucked in the blankets around the young girl's slender body. Coming to rest next to Rosie gently, Alana stroked her hair as she fell asleep, happy when Rosie cuddled into her curvier side as she slept. Alana wondered how she had so easily become so heavily caught up into Rosie's world, her last thought as her eyes finally shut.

"Good morning, sweetheart," Alana said, coming into the bedroom with coffee and bagels. She walked to the balcony windows and opened them, peering down onto the street that had come to life underneath them. She smiled to herself, thinking of how the paparazzi would go crazy to know that Rosie was sleepily waking up in her bed. Alana looked back and saw Rosie open her eyes and blink slowly, looking around to try and find Alana.

"Hey," Rosie said, sitting up and watching Alana light a cigarette.

"Howdy," Alana replied, winking at the starlet. She liked watching Rosie more than she wished she did and stayed out on the balcony as she watched her stretch her slim arms up and pull her hair into a messy ponytail. She had slept naked and walked her vulnerable body towards Alana, stopping when she got to the entrance to the balcony.

"Do you know how to make a million dollars in five seconds?" Rosie giggled, taking Alana's cigarette and walking naked out onto the balcony, making Alana smirk.

"Get back in here," Alana laughed, pulling Rosie into her and holding her naked body, shielding her from the street and pushing her back inside.

"I know how to make a billion darling," Alana teased, pushing Rosie onto the bed and jumping on top of her, pinning her arms above her head. Rosie's playful laughs quietened, and she began breathing nervously, making Alana grind her teeth and hop off her.

"What are you going to do today?" Alana said, taking a coffee and sipping it while looking at Rosie.

"You," Rosie said, slipping off the bed and getting onto her knees, pulling Alana forward by the top of her skirt and pulling it up before Alana could stop her.

"Whoa hey," Alana said as she felt Rosie's tongue taste her through her panties.

"Oh, baby, you don't have to," Alana stuttered between breaths, spreading her thighs and placing her hand on the back of Rosie's head.

"It feels like you want me too," Rosie laughed before sucking on Alana's pussy lips and pulling her panties to the side, sliding her tongue up and down Alana's slit. Alana closed her eyes and rolled her head back; she hadn't thought Rosie would be so good.

"You're wet, Mommy," Rosie said. Alana suddenly opened her eyes and cupped Rosie's chin before looking at her angrily in the eyes.

"What did you just call me?" She demanded making Rosie try to cower away, Alana making it impossible by her grip.

"Mommy," Rosie whispered, looking down and going red.

"Fuck, good girl," Alana said, pushing Rosie's mouth back as she stood over her, pushing her hot cunt against the young girl's face.

"Lick Mommy's pussy baby girl," Alana said, reaching down and slapping Rosie's tits and flicking her nipples. Rosie dipped her tongue into Alana's pussy, moaning as she tasted her juices as Alana began to rub her clit.

"Fuck," Alana moaned slowly as she grabbed a handful of Rosie's hair and pulled her head back, taking her mouth off her creaming pussy.

"I can't baby, I'm sorry," Alana said, gently wiping her pussy juices off Rosie's mouth, kissing her tenderly and pulling her to her feet. Alana readjusted her panties and skirt and sat on the edge of the bed with a very confused Rosie.

"Um, do I suck?" Rosie asked nervously.

"Coz I've never fucked a girl before so like, I don't know what the go is," Rosie started to say, stopping when she saw Alana shake her head.

"No baby, you don't suck at all! I don't want to take advantage of you," Alana said, making Rosie roll her eyes.

"I wish you did," Rosie said, going over to where her clothes were laying and getting dressed.

"I suppose that I should be grateful that you are so respectful or whatever, but seriously, do you know how many people want to fuck me, and you just turned me down like what the fuck," Rosie said. Alana let her rant and passed her a coffee as she walked towards the door.

"Do you think I don't want to fuck you? Is that what it felt like when I dripped in that pretty little mouth?" Alana said, taking Rosie by the hips and grinding into her, making Rosie soften her angry eyes.

"Then why don't you want me?" Rosie whined, letting Alana rub her breasts against Rosie's face as she was cuddled.

"I do want you. Though anyone can have this little thing, I want it for keeps baby girl. So until you give it all to Mommy, you can play with everyone but me. Think about it," Alana said, groping Rosie's pussy as she spoke, making her a moaning mess in her hands before kissing the top of her head and gently pushing her out the door and closing it behind her. Alana took a breath and sighed as she shook her head in disbelief that she had firstly, fell for Rosie, and secondly, stopped her slutty little mouth when she had been the best Alana had ever had in a long time.

Alana spent the rest of the day finishing Rosie's photos and getting multiple texts from Rosie in various positions. Her young firm body making

Alana edit her image to capture Rosie like the slut she wanted to be.

"Stop it," Alana said when Rosie answered her phone.

"Stop what?" Rosie giggled down the phone, making Alana smile.

"Stop sending me photos of you trying to win the award for the biggest whore of the year," Alana said firmly.

"Yes, Mommy," Rosie teased, making Alana have more ideas than she wished she did.

"Oh, baby girl, you don't want to start this game with me. Mommy doesn't play nice," Alana warned, making Rosie stop her giggling and go quiet on the phone.

"Yes, Mommy," was all that came after a few seconds, silence.

"I'm finished your photos. I think you'll like them; it's what you were after," Alana said, wanting to bring some professionalism back to the dynamic, but Rosie wasn't interested.

"What do you mean, you don't play nice?"

She questioned, making Alana roll her eyes.

"They are printed and framed to the specifications you requested, where am I dropping them off?" Alana said, ignoring Rosie's curiosity.

"That wasn't my question," Rosie replied. Alana thought for a minute before speaking again.

"You must be confused, little one; Mommy doesn't answer to you, ever. Tell me where you need them dropped off now," Alana said sternly, taking Rosie by surprise.

"5th Ave, there's a hotel there, I'll get someone to text you the address, I don't know the name of it," Rosie said before hanging up the phone, put out that Alana wasn't letting her have her way.

Chapter 4

The second week of Alana's trip was coming to an end, and she knew two things. The first was that Rosie hadn't messaged or called her since she had turned her down, and the second was that she was pretty sure she knew why. There had been newspaper articles written about it, morning TV programs talking about it, and social media had blown up over it. The series had been shown to the public before the auction, and it had all but broken the internet. With its only aim to seduce and tease, the media had analyzed it as though it would cure cancer. The only commonality that tied everyone's opinions together was the intensity in their feeling. They either loved it, or they hated it, and they pleaded their cases with equal enthusiasm. Calling Alana's work a modern-day masterpiece and a complete representation of a desperate millennial, Alana wondered how she would ever be able to move forward. She had stayed indoors, annoyed the paparazzi had been hounding her hotel since the piece had been unveiled.

Ordering room service for the third day in a row, Alana looked online to see if the photos were still trending when her phone rang.

"Hey, I was just thinking about you," Alana said before Rosie could speak.

"It's a bit crazy, right? I didn't think this would happen," Rosie said back, a smile escaping her voice. Alana was relieved that Rosie seemed unscathed by the brutal publicity.

"So, how are you holding up?" Alana asked nervously.

"The only way I know how," Rosie replied, making Alana curious.

"Meaning?" Alana prompted. Rosie sighed as if she knew that Alana wouldn't approve of her coping methods.

"I've been partying ever since they were unveiled, I'm not even sure what day it is," Rosie said leaving out the parts where she had done more drugs than her body could hold, drank her bar dry and if it weren't for her very loyal security she would have had the paparazzi photos to prove it.

"Oh," Alana replied, unsure of what to say.

"Well, I'm glad you're alright. Why are you calling me?" She added, not wanting Rosie to think she was judging her.

"I wanted to see if you wanted to come over," Rosie laughed.

"For what? Partying? Not my scene," Alana said, enjoying Rosie's giggle down the phone.

"No, not so much of a party, as more of a, um, softer kind of time," Rosie said, being very cryptic. Alana knew what Rosie wanted and gave a sideward smile as she thought.

"I don't know, from the sounds of things, you haven't been a very good girl," Alana said, hoping that she wasn't on the loudspeaker.

"Well, maybe I do deserve a punishment, then Mommy," Rosie replied, making Alana's eyes go wide.

"You couldn't handle Mommy's punishments, baby girl," Alana said, teasing her.

"Oh please, Mommy," Rosie said just before Alana hung up the phone. Sending Rosie a text instead, wanting her to read it over and over before she saw her.

Get in the shower, and make sure you're clean for me. I want you naked in bed when I see you; your sheets better be clean too. Take out a toy you want to play with and have it laying at the end of your bed. I'm going to push you today, sweet baby, love Mommy.

Alana was let into Rosie's house by her maid, who received a generous tip making the maid look confused at Alana.

"For your discretion," Alana said, looking the maid in the eyes who just nodded her head and pointed upstairs. Alana climbed the marble stairwell and walked along the hallway to Rosie's room, opening the door slowly.

"I'm in here, Mommy," Rosie excitedly said

when she saw Alana. Alana stopped and looked at Rosie, enjoying how easy it had been to get her naked and willing to be fucked. Closing the door and locking it behind her, Alana slowly made her way to the bed, climbing on top and eyeing Rosie predatorily.

"What a cute little girl," Alana said as she stroked Rosie's face lovingly, making her gasp when she firmly slapped her cheek.

"I told you Mommy was going to push you today, sweetheart," Alana said, taking the pink bunny Rosie was cuddling and gave her red cheek kisses with it.

"Good thing, bunny is here to kiss you better baby because Mommy isn't going to today," Alana said, getting up and going to her bag she had left at the door. She opened the bag, winking at Rosie, who just giggled and took out two black silk ties and a strap-on.

"I wonder what fun I can have with these," Alana teased as she dropped the ties on Rosie's body and began to fasten the harness of the strap-on, enjoying the knowledge that Rosie would have to cum several times before it would fit her tight pussy. Alana took the ties and gently tied Rosie's ankles together, rubbing her freshly shaven cunt softly, parting her pussy lips and spitting on her clit before moving up to her wrists.

"So you want to play with your nipple clamps today, little one?" Alana asked, securing them onto Rosie, making her moan and squirm around.

"Oh, you thought I'd be gentle? Silly little girl, you aren't listening to Mommy, are you?" Alana said, placing her larger hand on Rosie's neck and squeezing until she was gasping.

"Start playing with yourself little one, you'll want to get nice and wet for Mommy or what I'll do to you will hurt even more," Alana said taking Rosie's writing hand and tying it above her head, gently slapping her tits until Rosie was playing with herself at a pace Alana was satisfied with.

"Good girl," Alana said, sitting back and stroking the big black dildo she had claimed as her own. The black silicon of the cock glistened as Alana pushed it into Rosie's mouth, taking out her camera and photographing the compromised girl making her startle.

"Alana, don't," Rosie said, pulling back and refusing her cock. Alana laughed and sat back and took photos of Rosie until she merely lay still on her back.

"These are just for me, baby girl," Alana said, filling Rosie's mouth once again.

"Suck it, bitch," Alana commanded when Rosie tried to refuse her again, flicking the firm clamps on her nipples until she obeyed.

"Let me explain something to you, you pretty little slut, you're Mommy's plaything, and I am going to do whatever the fuck I want with you. If that means I want to take your photo, I'm going to fucking take your photo, and all that'll happen if you try to stop me is this," Alana said reaching behind her and slapping Rosie's pussy and roughly parted her pussy lips, fingering her with two fingers roughly as she screamed and moaned around Alana's cock.

"I know you'd take it. Little whores like you always do," Alana said as Rosie tried to match her thrusts, grinding into Alana's palm and sucking harder as Alana fucked her cunt and her mouth.

"Mommy I," Rosie started to say, stopping when Alana pulled out of her mouth and covered her lips with her hand.

"You'd better start with sorry, Mommy baby girl," Alana said, pushing Rosie's head back firmly until her eyes began to water. Raising an eyebrow and waiting for a response, Rosie nodded as Alana took her hand away.

"Sorry, Mommy," Rosie meekly said, making Alana smile. She lay down next to Rosie and pulled her into her, making her arms and legs stretch.

"Mommy's sweet baby. You're not so naughty now are you sweet girl," Alana said, taking a paci gag and securing it around the back of Rosie's head.

"Do you remember the safe words or actions, in this case, baby girl?" Alana asked Rosie as she stroked her hair and ran her fingernails up and down Rosie's back. Rosie smiled behind the gag and nodded her head before Alana kissed her forehead and placed her hand on her throat again.

"Good, then Mommy can get to work," Alana said, squeezing tightly on Rosie's throat and spitting into her hand. She began rubbing her cock again, slapping it against Rosie's cheek until she had covered both cheeks with her spit. Alana moved down to Rosie's thighs and gripped them firmly, pulling them apart before spitting on Rosie's already wet pussy. Alana smirked when she saw that Rosie had stopped playing with herself.

"Did I fucking say to stop?" Alana said, using both hands to firmly slap Rosie's thighs until her handprints had made them burn red, and Rosie squirm uncontrollably trying to escape.

"You're mine bitch, and you aren't going anywhere," Alana explained as she stretched Rosie's pussy and forcibly entered her, making her squeal and moan. Thrusting into her aggressively,

Alana watched as the young girl became a hot mess in front of her, reminding her of the French girl she had used less than a month ago. Losing her train of thought, Alana shook her head and looked down at the famous girl's fuck doll-like body and reached for her un-tied wrist, deciding it was time to secure that as well.

"Come here, darling," Alana said, letting her affection for the girl escape her voice. But Rosie didn't notice; she was too busy having her fifth orgasm as Alana plowed her young cunt with a vengeance while she tied her wrist above her head. Alana couldn't care less how many orgasms Rosie had or if she even had any at all, Rosie's pleasure was of zero consequence to Alana. She was just there for Alana's pleasure. Alana smirked as she held Rosie's pelvis down, her hands on either side of the young girl's body and watched as her tummy was pushed out by the huge cock Alana was happily destroying her with the force she had used on Rosie at the beginning now less than necessary as her wet pussy took Alana's long strokes while she was slapped over and over. Rosie's slender body turning red as Alana marked her soft skin.

"I want you to finish me baby girl," Alana said, suddenly breaking her rhythm and pulling down the gag as she sat on top of Rosie's mouth as her last orgasm hit, shooting down Rosie's throat as she squirted taking Rosie by surprise.

"Swallow Mommy baby girl," Alana said lovingly while grinding deeply on Rosie's mouth, enjoying using her as if she were a common street whore.

Chapter 5

Alana woke up to Rosie's hair tickling her face, and she slowly opened her eyes, letting them adjust to the moonlight streaming through the windows and felt the familiar hollow of her heart she tried so hard to fill. She lifted her arms to the ceiling and checked her phone. It was only 2:30 in the morning; she knew the bars and clubs would still be open and slowly crept out of bed as to not wake Rosie. Taking a cigarette and a bottle of whiskey from the nightstand, Alana made her way out to the balcony and into the cold air of the night. Watching the garden lights flicker and the blue lights of the lagoon-style pool, Alana sat and watched the darkness. She could feel it. The evil she had outran but never been able to out-grow. The memories haunting her like the wind, always there, however calm or fierce. She popped the cork of the bottle and let it fall onto the floor as she tilted her head back to drink the liquid that did nothing but burn her throat before she lit her cigarette and blew the smoke into the night. The stars that she knew where there weren't seen from the cloudy night sky, and she wondered what would happen if she just stopped trying. What the sound would be like if she were to fall to the ground if anyone would miss her. Drinking again, she could feel the alcohol start to warm her body and pulse through her veins.

"What are you doing?" Rosie said, taking Alana by surprise and ripping her out of a memory she wished didn't belong to her.

"Nothing," Alana said, trying to hide her vulnerability, surprised when Rosie looked at her as though she saw it too.

"Mind if I join you?" Rosie asked seriously, taking the bottle gently from Alana's fingers.

"You can do whatever you want this is your house," Alana said, putting her guard up and making Rosie look at her with a seriousness Alana hadn't seen before.

"Do you want to share this with me?" Alana asked, offering the cigarette to Rosie, who smiled and took a drag before giving it back.

"You know, they think I'm just this stupid rich kid that has everything I want," Rosie said, drinking deeply until she coughed and handed the bottle back to Alana.

"Aren't you?" Alana questioned playfully, making Rosie laugh.

"No. I'm not stupid, and I have never got everything I want. I want peace, I've tried, but money can't buy that," Rosie replied, and Alana was surprised that they were having this conversation. *Maybe I fucked the fake out of her*, Alana thought to herself smirking as she remembered how Rosie had ridden her cock like a bitch on heat.

"I don't think you're stupid," Alana said, wondering where the conversation would go.

"I know you don't, that's why I'm here," Rosie said bluntly before looking Alana in the eye.

"Don't care what they say about you, do

you?" Rosie questioned, looking at Alana curiously, referring to the mass media attention and criticism that had been placed on both of them like a crown of thorns. Alana tried to suppress her smirk before she looked up at Rosie.

"No, I don't. But I also don't want to be in the limelight like you do," Alana replied, seeing that Rosie wasn't satisfied with her answer.

"But you were hiding before this, who are you hiding from?" Rosie pressed.

"Now why would I tell you that?" Alana teased, pulling Rosie onto her lap and holding her tightly.

"Because I see it, I see you," Rosie whispered in Alana's ear, almost bringing her to tears instantly.

"You surprise me, little one. It's from a long time ago," Alana replied, burying her face into Rosie's sweet-smelling body, her warmth comforting Alana.

"And yet here you are," Rosie said, wrapping her arms around Alana's head, bringing her face into her breasts.

"You're such a baby," Rosie teased, making Alana suddenly laugh before sitting back and wiping her tears away.

"You want to know what haunts me?" Alana said, reaching for her phone. Rosie got up and went to sit on the opposite chair and waited for Alana to find what she was looking for.

"Her name was Silva. We went to high school together. She was going to be a lawyer. I was going to be a doctor," Alana began before taking another sip of the whiskey. Alana passed her phone to Rosie, who looked at the girl, clearly younger than she was. Her youthful smile and carefree soul emanating from the core of her being as she held her arms up to the sky and laughed with the universe. Rosie was surprised that such energy could be captured in a mere photo. She looked up from the phone and continued to sit quietly and gave Alana the time she needed to find the words to tell her story.

"She was my, my first, and if I'm honest, my

only love," Alana said nervously, looking at Rosie.

"It's OK; I knew this was never love," Rosie said, making Alana smile in relief.

"We were getting ready for our prom at her house when three men broke into the house," Alana said, stopping and looking blankly into the distance of the night. Rosie felt her stomach tighten because she already knew the rest of the story; most girls would.

"They had guns; we did what they said. By the time they left, Silva was hardly breathing, and I had to crawl to her neighbor's house to call the police because they had cut the electricity," Alana said, stopping to look at Rosie, who was looking at the ground.

"When I went back to the house, Silva had made her way to the front door. She kissed me goodbye, and I felt her last breath on my lips and watched as her lips smiled for the last time," Alana said as tears poured down her cheeks as she silently cried unstoppable tears. Rosie was speechless and dipped her head as the story so fucking familiar to hundreds of thousands of women was once again told by a broken heart who had to rebuild her life after someone tried to take it from her.

"When will they stop destroying us," Rosie said as tears fell from her our eyes and onto the tiles.

"I don't know, sweetheart," Alana said, breathing in deeply as the air changed and began to warm, the sunrise lighting their faces.

"You made it," Rosie said, looking happily at Alana.

"What?" Alana asked, finishing off the whiskey.

"You made it through the night," Rosie said, standing up and walking over to Alana, who held her like she was her life raft.

"For now," Alana said, her tears welling up in her eyes again.

"Forever," Rosie said, kissing her tears away.

"I don't think I can take the pain forever,

sweetheart," Alana replied, laughing in disbelief at the mountain she knew she was climbing.

"I'll help you," Rosie said, feeling her heartbeat faster than she wished it would.

Chapter 6

"Well, what the fuck am I supposed to do with you now?" Alana playfully asked Rosie over breakfast only a few hours later. They had gone to a close-by coffee shop and sat away from the windows. Rosie laughed to herself as she watched the other customers choose window seats without having to think of the headlines that would accompany their morning.

"I don't know, can you even see this going anywhere?" Rosie replied as she sipped her triple shot iced caramel Frappuccino. They sat in silence and watched the world around them with a distance like watching a movie. People were rushing in and impatiently waiting for their takeaway orders and others that were typing furiously on laptops with a pile of espresso cups collecting on their table. Alana watched as Rosie looked around at the happy couples stealing kisses in the morning sun and the newspaper delivery man dropping off the coffee shop's order.

"I have thought about retiring, you know," Rosie suddenly said over the sound of a loud coffee machine. The smell of burnt bread drifted towards them, and they laughed at the trainee who was frantically trying to fix his mistake.

"What would you do instead?" Alana asked, finishing her black coffee. Rosie just shrugged her shoulders.

"It's not like I do anything now anyway, I kinda just want to slip out of the limelight," Rosie explained. Alana understood why Rosie wanted to run away. If she had every public moment under constant criticism, she would also want to hideaway. She hadn't truly noticed the pain in Rosie's eyes until this moment, and she wondered how she could carry such heavy sadness.

"You've done what you've wanted this far, why stop now?" Alana said, bringing a smile to Rosie's lips.

"Because a lot of people will lose a lot of

money if I stop. I can hear the blackmail now," Rosie replied, motioning to the waitress before ordering another coffee.

"I made the mistake of creating a scandal the first time I wanted out, it backfired and flung me even further into the spotlight," Rosie laughed, Alana was happy she could see the humor in it.

"Like, what are you doing for the next few weeks?" Rosie suddenly said as the morning sun poured into the coffee shop. Alana smiled, excited to see what Rosie was planning.

"Nothing. Nothing that I can't palm off or put off, what did you have in mind?" Alana found herself saying. Rosie took a deep breath and held it before exhaling dramatically.

"Let's go, let's get the fuck out of here. You can work from anywhere, and it's not like we would run out of cash, let's go," Rosie said, taking Alana by surprise. Alana looked at Rosie and knew that she would leave with or without her, and she had to admit, life was a lot more fun with Rosie.

"OK," Alana replied as Rosie took her hand

and held it with a shaky hand as tears started to pour down her face.

"It'll be alright little one," Alana said, making Rosie laugh through her tears as she stood and held Alana's hand, walking through the coffee shop and fighting the urge to let go as people began to recognize her. Rosie's world turned in slow motion as she saw people begin to take out their phones and take photos of her and Alana, following them out onto the street. The excitement of the people who began to circle them made it difficult to walk, and Alana had to push people out of the way so they could make their way back to Rosie's mansion. Rosie gripped Alana's hand, but as a wave of paparazzi swarmed, Rosie felt Alana get swept out of her reach, and she was there, surrounded by strangers all clicking and yelling questions and opinions at her. Rosie frantically looked for Alana in the mass of people circling, turning around to try and find the hand that had steadied her.

"What?! What do you want from me?!"

Rosie screamed as she saw Alana burst through the crowd knocking some people to the ground as she grabbed Rosie's hand once again and pulled her close kissing her forehead and grabbing a camera and throwing it onto the road before taking out her gun and pointing it to the crowd who backed up instantly.

"Fuck off, will you?" Alana calmly said while holding Rosie. They turned and begun to walk back along the street, toward the mansion that was a mere five blocks away.

"Where you going to use that?" Rosie quietly asked, still holding Alana's hand. Rosie hadn't realized Alana had or even carried a gun, but surprisingly it didn't scare her.

"Nope, there's no bullets in it," Alana laughed, making Rosie cuddle her arm as they turned the corner.

"Thanks, Mommy," Rosie said, resting her head on Alana's shoulder as they walked, Alana winking at her as she felt the ache of her broken heart being put back together by the most unlikely of heroes.

"You used some very grown-up words back there, baby," Alana said, referring to the vicious manner Rosie had spoken to the crowd only moments before.

"So did you," Rosie replied, kissing Alana's arm.

"Yes, but I don't think I like my little one speaking like that," Alana said, making Rosie laugh.

"Yours?" She questioned, twirling out of Alana's arms and coming to stand in front of her.

"Oh, you don't feel claimed? That can be changed," Alana said, taking Rosie's hand firmly and walking her faster back down the street.

"What are you going to do, make me color some pictures or something?" Rosie said teasingly.

"No that would be so stupid, you're far too big for that, but you're not too big to be bent over my knee and spanked, diapered until you can't hold it anymore and bottle-fed while Mommy gives you little kisses on your nose," Alana said making Rosie stop walking and look at her blankly.

"Really?" She asked, her world stopping as she looked at Alana like she had just answered all of her deepest questions, shared her darkest secrets, and saw her in her truest form. Alana looked back at Rosie, wondering if this girl in front of her was someone she could commit too or not.

"Really," Alana said as Rosie jumped into her arms and kissed her mouth, forgetting the rules that she had lived by for the last three years.

Chapter 7

"Where do you want to go?" Rosie said, sitting on Alana's hotel bed, flicking through a list of countries on Alana's laptop.

"Honestly, I don't care. You can decide baby girl," Alana said, coming over to kiss Rosie before going back to packing her things.

"In Europe? Austria is nice this time of year?" Rosie asked Alana, who just nodded her head and kept packing. She had never been and was surprised how willing she was just to let go and jump into the mess that was the world with Rosie.

"Great, I'll just ring Jack," Rosie said, taking out her phone.

"Who's Jack?" Alana asked from the bathroom. She looked at herself in the mirror and wondered what Rosie saw in her. She was naturally beautiful, but the years of her life and the long nights of torment had worn their presence onto her face.

"My pilot," Rosie casually replied, making Alana laugh at herself and shake her head at how nonchalant Rosie was about flying private.

Alana tried to play it cool as they approached the private jet and bit her bottom lip to try and stop herself smiling like an idiot, but Rosie saw it all.

"Yeah, it is pretty cool, huh?" Rosie said as the car stopped. They got out, and Alana was impressed that Rosie had achieved so much of what most people deemed success. Alana followed Rosie over the tarmac and felt like she was in a movie as she climbed the stairs of the plane, reaching out and placing both her hands on Rosie's hips and pulled her back slightly.

"You're a clever girl," Alana whispered in Rosie's ear as she held her from behind, making Rosie turn in her arms and kiss her passionately, running her fingers through Alana's thick black hair and giggling as Alana wrapped her arms around her waist as Rosie melted.

"Come on, Mommy," Rosie whispered, making Alana smirk and let her go as they boarded the plane.

"This is insane; you do know that, right?" Alana said, walking up and down the aisle, holding Champaign in one hand and biting her other thumb. Rosie laughed and looked out the window. They had been flying for three hours and were over the ocean. The glistening blue looked like someone had dropped diamonds over the surface, and Rosie exhaled deeply, catching Alana's attention.

"What is it?" She questioned coming to sit next to Rosi, who didn't bother to turn around but kept looking out the window. Alana put her glass down and reached out to turn Rosie's face to her.

"Hey," Alana said with concern as a tear rolled down Rosie's face.

"Nothing," Rosie replied, making Alana roll her eyes.

"Don't lie to Mommy," Alana said, making Rosie laugh despite herself.

"What are we even doing?" Rosie said defeatedly. Alana thought for a minute. She was on the private jet of a 22-year-old who had convinced the world they should pay for her existence, on their way to Austria, and said girl liked calling her Mommy.

"We are on a rather big adventure, sweetheart," Alana said, stopping when she felt Rosie's hand reach for hers.

"I want to love you, Alana," Rosie said, sadly looking down.

"I know you do, darling. I'm sorry I can't love you the way you want me too. But I can do this," Alana said, getting up and pulling Rosie up with her before laying her down on the sofa on the other side of the plane. Alana lay down next to Rosie and rested on her elbow, stroking Rosie's cheek and looking at her tenderly.

"I can look after you. I can hold you closer than you've ever been held, and I can protect you with a ferociousness that even frightens me. I can promise you that I will stay as long as you want me and that my arms will always be open for you. You can trust me with this," Alana said as she placed her hand on Rosie's heart and looked down on her face before bending her head and kissing her gently.

"But I don't know how to rebuild the parts of me that feel," Alana stated honestly.

"And I would give those to you as well if I did sweetheart. You can have all of me that I still have left, and you can trust that I won't leave you," Alana said, dropping her body to rest against Rosie's who snuggled into her.

"I love you, Alana," Rosie whispered as she held Alana's arm and traced the lines of her face, tracing her soft fingertips over Alana's lips and the bridge of her nose.

"You have all of me, sweetheart," Alana replied, her eyes smiling as she caught herself laughing.

"I can't believe this is happening. You are

such a big girl for such a baby," Alana teased, bringing their conversation into a lighter note.

"So are you," Rosie said, giggling as Alana scoffed.

"Don't think for a second I will not bend you over my knee and spank you right here sweetheart," Alana said, staring into Rosie's wild eyes. Rosie's gaze was full of daring and mischief as Alana decided it was time to remind her that just because she had some demons, didn't make her any less of Rosie's Mommy. Grabbing Rosie by her upper arm, Alana pulled her up and over her lap, pinning her down with her forearm.

"Don't make such a fuss or captain Jack might want to come and see what all the fuss is about baby girl," Alana said, covering Rosie's mouth with her hand and rubbing her ass under her skirt.

"No panties, I should have just assumed," Alana laughed, cupping her pussy from behind and teasing her clit as her moans where muffled.

"Such a wet and horny little one, aren't you.

That's how I like my girl, always ready and willing to be taken," Alana almost moaned, getting turned on as Rosie spread her thighs and reached back to spread her ass for Alana.

"Is that where you want it, little one?" Alana asked, reaching into her bag and taking out a slim vibrator and pushing it into Rosie's mouth.

"Get it wet sugar," Alana commanded before spitting on it and sliding it into Rosie's ass and turning it on, making Rosie dip her head forward and arch her back as Alana filled her.

"How am I supposed to keep it in there without you wearing any panties. Good thing Mommy is prepared isn't it baby girl," Alana said mostly to herself as Rosie was busy squirming on her lap. Alana took out a Chasity belt and slid it up Rosie's thighs before standing her up and locking it in place before Rosie knew what was happening.

"Mommy," Rosie whined and straddled Alana's soft thigh before rubbing herself on top of it, trying to make her orgasm hit her like she craved.

"No, that's all you're getting little one, oh, that and this," Alana said, taking a diaper out of her bag and making Rosie gasp.

"You didn't think you were so big that I'd leave you uncovered, did you?" Alana said, standing up and looking down at Rosie.

"Are you going to be a good girl for Mommy?" Alana asked, pulling on the top of the belt, making Rosie bite her bottom lip and nod her head with excitement in her eyes.

"Good, come here then, baby girl," Alana said, pulling Rosie to the floor and putting the diaper over the top of the belt that was securing the vibrator.

"Pretty girl," Alana said, running her hands over the diapered girl in front of her.

"You know, I'll have to be out of this when we land Alana," Rosie said nervously, breaking their play, worried about what the future held. Alana raised her eyebrow.

"Mommy," Alana corrected gently as she shook her head and pulled Rosie back down next to her.

"Of course, baby girl. You can trust Mommy," she added, cradling Rosie in her arms.

Chapter 8

Alana and Rosie rented a cabin in the mountains outside a small village in the Austrian Alps. Alana had taken to working in the mornings as Rosie slept, taking on online orders, which helped to create a routine they enjoyed following. Rosie tied up her life, telling her people that she wouldn't be taking on any new products or endorsements and selling off three of her homes to buy herself out of two of her contracts she had with big clothing labels. The internet went wild with speculation as to what her mental state was but tucked away in the mountains with Alana had her more stable than she had ever been.

"Hi baby girl," Alana said, coming into their bedroom to see that Rosie had woken up and was happily sucking on her paci and playing with the stuffies that despite Alana's best attempts, always seemed to make their way into their bed.

"I thought I told you to put these away last night?" Alana questioned playfully, making Rosie giggle and roll around in bed.

"Come here, little one," Alana said, placing her laptop down and getting back into bed with Rosie. It was winter, and the snow had fallen knee-deep, making walking on the mountains difficult, so Alana and Rosie had taken to staying indoors, except for their shopping days.

"I think we need to go into town darling, or you're little tummy will be hungry soon," Alana said, running her hands over Rosie's fluffy white onesie and playfully biting her neck making Rosie giggle and push Alana away.

"Mommy!" Rosie squealed before Alana stopped and stood her up.

"Come on darling, Mommy needs to get you dressed so we can go," Alana said taking Rosie's hand and leading her to the cupboard, opening it up and looking at what she wanted Rosie in today.

"This will look cute," Alana said, taking out

red plaid winter trousers and black high-top ankle boots, a long-sleeve white thermal top, and a black puffer jacket. Rosie shook her head no as Alana began to dress her, making Alana roll her eyes and grip Rosie's chin, forcing her to look at her in the eyes.

"No?" Alana questioned, making Rosie look sideward and stop refusing.

"This one, Mommy," Rosie said, pointing to a pair of pink pants instead.

"Please, Mommy. Where are your manners, little one?" Alana said, slapping Rosie's bottom firmly.

"That's not how you ask, and you know it. Don't be a bad girl for Mommy; you know what happens if you are a naughty baby girl," Alana said, taking out the cane she had used on Rosie a week earlier. Rosie began to suck her thumb, and Alana knew she would have no trouble with her for the rest of the day. Alana dressed Rosie, pulling her pants over her diaper and zipping up her jacket before she got herself dressed. They had been in

Austria for a month and knowing they would only be here for another 3 weeks, Alana didn't buy the week supply of groceries she had done previously, instead she decided to only buy for a couple of days and settled with the plan that they would eat out for the rest of their stay.

"No, put it back baby, we don't need it," Alana said to Rosie, who tried to put a big bag of candy in the shopping cart. Rosie pouted but obeyed, forcing Alana to try and suppress her smile. She loved having Rosie as hers. It hadn't felt the way Alana had first thought it would. Rosie was different from her. With everyone else, she was the playful, cheeky slut who would be happily gaging to be fucked by anyone who wanted her. With Alana, she was calm, thoughtful, observant, and sensual, and Alana loved that Rosie had those qualities and that they were all hers.

"Sweetie?" Alana asked Rosie, who was holding a magazine in her hands. Alana looked over Rosie's shoulder and saw what Rosie was looking at. *Young entrepreneur assumed dead*, read the headline with Rosie's photo under it.

"They think I'm dead?" Rosie said in a confused voice that Alana didn't know how to read. Alana waited for a response to come and held her breath in nervous anticipation.

"That is so rude!" Rosie laughed, putting the magazine down and walking off to get the milk Alana has told her to get. Alana smiled to herself as her heart was filled with pride at how far her baby girl had come. From the sensitive girl that was scared of the world to the woman who was comfortable in her skin and comfortable with what she needed to be happy.

Fuck. My turn, Alana thought as she got in the car and listened to Rosie's story about a dog she had just seen that was as big as a pony.

"What are you doing, Mommy?" Rosie asked, coming up behind Alana, who sat in the sunroom typing on her laptop. Rosie had gone for a walk that morning, and Alana took the time to begin to write about the things that haunted her. *If my baby can manage to sort her head out, maybe I can do the same*, Alana had thought while fucking Rosie the night before. Alana hadn't heard Rosie come back into the cabin and was startled, jumping and getting the hiccups, which just made Rosie laugh.

"Mommy, you are so silly, look, I got you a flower!" Rosie said, presenting the yellow petaled flower to Alana, who bit her bottom lip.

"You're a little bit cute do you know that?" Alana said, pulling Rosie onto her lap and reading out the first paragraph she had written.

"She howled from the depths of her soul without regard for who could hear. The long journey to the top of the mountain had left her breathless, the pads of her paws sore and tender. 'Don't feel sorry for me,' she whispered to the small hedgehog who came out to see what the dark shaggy fur was that sat outside her burrow. 'Feel sorry for them,' she said, looking down the path she had just forged. Through stone and dirt, she had dug her path. It was deep, deep enough to hide a wolf as it made its way behind her and oh how they had. Snapping at her heels, biting down on her hunches, they had only made her ascent faster, all the while trying to slow her down. And when she had finally reached the top, turning in one quick motion, she pushed them down the steep slope and watched as they tumbled and fell until she could sit safely on her perch. The hedgehog knew none of this; she hadn't come in on that chapter of the young wolf's story, she had only seen the victory and wondered why the wolf had refused to allow another on the top with her. 'Won't you get lonely?' She asked. 'No,' replied the wolf who turned to the rising moon and smiled as she saw a black figure moving towards her. 'I didn't climb this mountain for me, I climbed it for her,' the wolf said as another wolf greeted her and together they began to howl to the stars and moon that decorated the night's sky," Alana read, remaining silent and waiting when she finished seeing what Rosie would say.

"Silva?" Rosie asked. Alana liked that Rosie never made her feel bad for still being in that room with Silva no matter where in the world she physically was, but this time, Rosie was wrong.

"No," Alana whispered, looking down and smiling to herself. For this first time, she had been able to feel a glimmer of something else. As though the door to her heart had been unlocked and left open, letting her move in and out of the space.

"Not this time. I want to love you," Alana said quietly as Rosie took her hand tenderly and kissed her cheek.

"I know you do," Rosie replied, her words not escaping Alana, who laughed as Rosie replied with the same words Alana had only a month ago.

Chapter 9

"Mommy?" Rosie said, coming back into the cabin on the day they were meant to leave. Alana and Rosie had decided that it was best to head back to the States and build their new life together there. They had both decided that it was too complicated to try and stay in Austria, and with Rosie's career slowing down they were both excited to get settled in New York. That's what Rosie thought was going to happen, but walking through the empty cabin, her heart began to scream words she didn't want to hear. Alana was gone. Her bags that had been packed near the door weren't there anymore, the toys that Rosie had left unpacked where all there except for the bunny that she often cuddled with, in Alana's arms and a letter was left on top of her suitcase.

I numbed it with everything that I could find darling — alcohol, sex, money, success. I stayed away from drugs; you've got to have your limits, right?! I see the sort of people who couldn't brace up, and I'm glad weakness was never an option for me, I don't think it's in my nature, but it is probably just a firm conditioning I refuse to shake. What do you want me to say? That I was sad, lonely, scared. That it felt like breathing for the first time when I would get lost in your touch and that nothing has made me feel as alive since. It is love I find so fucking painful; I'm very happy enjoying a girl for a while, but love is just too much for me to be able to let sink in. I knew I had a choice I knew I could have just let you go, but I wanted to let you love me, I wanted to love you, but it's just too painful. I'm sorry, baby girl, take care, Alana.

Rosie froze, speechless. She sat down next to her bags and cried for the first time in ten years, crying her heart out and feeling smaller and more worthless than she had ever felt in her life.

Alana had flown back to Paris and spent the next three weeks getting ritualistically drunk and looking up at the ceiling of a cheap hotel. The days of Rosie spun in her head, the days of Silva always interrupted them, hearing the sound of gunshots in her nightmares startling her awake.

"She's better off without me," Alana said out loud to herself as she stood and looked around her darkroom for a bottle with anything left in it. The bunny she had taken from Rosie had long lost her scent of perfume and now reeked of bourbon and cigarettes. A knock came from the door, and Alana stumbled to the door, opening it slowly.

"Hi, you wanna let me in?" The woman the Alana had forgotten she had ordered hours before said, standing in front of her. Alana wiped her eyes and shrugged her shoulders and walked back into the bedroom and fell on the bed.

"Money is on the counter," Alana said, breathing deeply and drinking the last of the bourbon she had found. The woman thought for a minute before coming to sit on the bed with Alana.

"What the fuck is the matter with you?" She suddenly said, making Alana's closed eyes open slowly.

"What?" Alana replied, unsure of what the woman was telling her.

"You're Alana Shummer, aren't you? You are with Rosie. What the fuck are you doing here like this?" The woman said, making Alana mad.

"I didn't pay for a fucking lecture, did I bitch?" She said, getting up to rest on her elbows.

"Well, it looks like you need one," The woman said, going to the windows and drawing the curtains back, making Alana squint.

"Tell me what the fuck has happened to get you like this?" The woman said, slapping Alana's face firmly when Alana started her rebuttal.

"Did I stutter, bitch?" The woman said confidently, making Alana laugh.

"Guess not," Alana said, sobering up quickly and sitting up, crossing her legs and looking at the woman for the first time.

"I couldn't give her what she needed. She needed love; I couldn't give her that. She's better off without me, the end," Alana explained to the frowning woman.

"So, are you finished lying to yourself?" The woman said, crossing her arms over her chest and waiting. Alana rolled her eyes and dramatically lay back down in bed.

"From what I've seen, Rosie had never been happier than when she was with you, didn't you guys go to some retreat or something together? You even protected her from the paparazzi. Have you seen how she's doing? She needs you more now than ever," The woman said, piquing Alana's curiosity.

"What do you mean?" Alana asked, concern in her voice.

"She's been taken to hospital, she broke down on a talk show, and she just sat there, crying, it went viral," The woman said, taking out her phone and finding the video of the interview Rosie came undone on. Handing it to Alana, Alana watched as the girl she had called hers cried as her heart broke in the most invasive manner possible.

"Why did you show me that?" Alana said

quietly, handing the woman her phone back.

"Because it looks like you could use more than just a fuck. You need a friend and a shower, come on," The woman said, taking Alana's hand and leading her into the shower, turning the water on and taking off Alana's clothes. The woman sat on the floor as Alana showered for the first time in days and watched as the bathroom steamed up as Alana let the hot water pour over her body.

"You can't burn out whatever it is that haunts you," The woman said, standing up and turning the water off. She passed Alana a towel as Alana reached for her packet of cigarettes.

"No," The woman said, slapping Alana's hand away. Alana raised an eyebrow at the woman who just laughed.

"I said no," The woman repeated, taking the cigarettes from the packet and breaking them in half.

"It's a filthy habit. You deserve better," The woman said to Alana, who, for the first time, let someone have control over her.

"What am I even meant to say to her?" Alana said as she got dressed in clean clothes and began cleaning the hotel room.

"Sorry, might be a good start. I imagine you've shattered her trust, so get ready for a backlash," The woman said, watching as Alana tidied and began packing.

"I'm going to call her," Alana said more to herself than the woman who nodded her head and sat down on the couch.

"Um," Alana said, wanting privacy and making the woman laugh as she got up and took the money from the counter.

"Good luck, darling. Be better," The woman said as she waved goodbye with the envelope of cash Alana had set aside for her.

Alana took a deep breath before clicking on Rosie's name, her photo covering Alana's phone screen as she called.

"Hello?" Rosie's voice quietly said, her vulnerability making Alana lost for words.

"I'm sorry," Alana said, matching the quiet

intensity of Rosie's voice. Silence echoed down the phone, but Rosie spoke first.

"You don't have to do this. I don't need you," she said, lying to herself.

"I know," Alana said, letting Rosie try and believe it.

"Then what do you want? Haven't you taken enough of me?" Rosie said, feeling anger begin to boil within her.

"I need help, Rosie," Alana said, admitting to her flaws for the first time in her life.

"Well, there's an empty bed here next to mine," Rosie said, laughing despite herself.

"I'll be there in a day," Alana said excitedly.

"Rosie?" Alana quickly added.

"Yep," Rosie said defensively.

"I'm sorry I broke your heart. Let me try and fix it?" Alana asked, biting her tongue as she almost slipped on the words.

"I can't say if I'll stay, but I'll let you try," Rosie said, hanging up the phone and placing her phone on her chest, breathing deeply as happy tears rolled down her cheeks.

"So, what am I supposed to do with you now?" Rosie said three weeks later upon seeing Alana standing in front of her. They had decided to meet at a back street art gallery after spending countless hours talking on the phone.

"Rosie," Alana said, becoming speechless and looked down at her feet, intimidated by the now powerful woman who stood in front of her.

"You had plenty to say before, do you want a pen and paper, would that be easier for you?!" Rosie angrily said, fire burning in her eyes, pain flooding her blood. Alana looked up and frowned.

"I never meant to hurt you," she said quietly, only enraging Rosie.

"What the fuck did you think it would do? You come in, take me in, make me feel for the first time, and then just bail?" Rosie yelled before walking out of the gallery, Alana, in tow.

"I'm sorry!" Alana yelled back at her, causing Rosie to stop and turn on her heel.

"Yeah, I get that, what I don't get is why," Rosie said, pacing back and forth on the graveled driveway out the back of the gallery. Alana didn't know how to reply, so she just stood there, watching her life turn in slow motion.

"You need help, Alana," Rosie said quietly, her expression changing from rage to love. She shook her head and half laughed, surprised that she was able to have this kind of conversation.

"You need help, or anti-depressants or Jesus, just something, anything. I thought we were happy; I thought you were happy," Rosie said, stepping closer to Alana, who felt littler than she had ever felt in her life.

"I know," Alana said softly, a tear escaping when she felt Rosie's hand on her cheek.

"Then let me help you, baby," Rosie said, making Alana laugh.

"You're still the baby, I don't care how sad I am I'm still your Mommy," Alana said without thinking, her eyes going wide as she heard what she had just said. Rosie thought for a moment before shaking her head no.

"You aren't anymore, Alana, well, not yet anyway. Maybe in the future, but not right now. I need to be able to trust you again; I need you to be better," Rosie said despite wanting Alana to be hers again desperately. Alana nodded, understanding the situation before smiling a cheeky smile.

"Guess I better see a shrink or something then. I have big plans for you, baby girl," Alana said, making Rosie laugh and hug her tightly.

"I don't want to love you as I do," Rosie whispered into Alana's chest as Alana held her. The sky turned dark as storm clouds came overhead and began lightly raining on the pair as they held each other, neither wanting to be the first to let go.

"Shall we go?" Rosie said to Alana, who nodded her head and slowly stepped back from Rosie, who just laughed.

"No, I mean, shall we go back to mine. I don't want to be alone tonight," Rosie said, holding out her hand beaming when Alana took her hand in hers and started running to her car as the sky suddenly burst, and large raindrops fell hard from the sky. Sitting wet in the car, Rosie reached over to wipe Alana's face catching her off guard.

"Hey," Alana laughed, becoming serious when she saw Rosie's face.

"I missed you. Will you get help?" She said as Alana turned the ignition and drove out of the car park.

"Yeah, I don't want to be that person for you or for me anymore. I near couldn't live with myself for those weeks. It got ugly," Alana confessed as Rosie took her hand in both of hers.

"How did you get out of it? Why did you want to come back to me?" Rosie questioned, looking out the window as Alana drove through the rain. Alana thought back to the night she had been given a reality check from the working girl she had paid and laughed, remembering how she had been ridiculously lovely.

"A friend talked me out of my bender. I'm

grateful because after I learned that you weren't doing well like I had thought you would go without me, I realized I needed to come back," Alana said, pulling over under a bridge and locking the doors.

"So, you thought that I *needed* you?" Rosie said, crossing her arms over her chest and pouting.

"Well, didn't you?" Alana said, amused and placing her hand on Rosie's thigh, slowly reaching under her skirt.

"Yes," Rosie said, feeling Alana stroke her pussy through her sheer panties.

"I thought so," Alana said, grabbing at Rosie, who moved to be straddling Alana's thighs as Alana put her seat back and held the back of Rosie's head as Rosie kissed her passionately, biting her lip hard.

"Ouch, baby!" Alana yelled, making Rosie giggle.

"Now we are even," Rosie said, licking her lips, tasting Alana's blood. Alana raised an eyebrow and tried to get up but was stopped by Rosie, who placed her hand on Alana's chest and pushed her back.

"I'm in control today Mommy," Rosie said, taking two fist fulls of Alana's T-shirt and ripping it open from the top.

"Not if you are going to make me look like bears have attacked me," Alana said, rolling Rosie onto her back and tearing her panties off.

"Hey, slow down, it's not as though I'm going anywhere," Rosie teased, making Alana blush.

"Yeah, sorry about that," Alana said, slowing down and kissing Rosie lovingly.

"I want you to be gentle with me, Mommy," Rosie whispered, enjoying the feel of Alana's full weight on top of her. Alana reached between Rosie's thighs and smiled as her wet pussy juices laced her fingers.

"You're always so ready, baby girl," Alana said, sliding into Rosie and making her moan in pleasure. Rosie closed her eyes and bit her bottom lip before shaking her head and pushing Alana off.

"No, Mommy, I don't want to," Rosie said,

her eyes looking afraid that Alana would be angry. Alana took her fingers out of Rosie and looked at her with concern.

"Did I hurt you, baby?" Alana asked, letting Rosie get up and move to the passenger seat, watching as she put her clothes back on.

"No, I just don't want sex, I kinda just want your cuddles right now," Rosie said, looking down and making Alana frown.

"You don't ever have to be worried about asking for what you need, little one, come on let's get you home and settled so you can cuddle with Mommy," Alana said, reaching for her jacket in the back seat.

"But first, I think I need to cover up," Alana joked, zipping her jacket up before she pulled out from under the bridge and back onto the road.

Chapter10

Alana smiled as she drove up the familiar driveway of Rosie's mansion home, stopping by the water fountain near the front door. It was late afternoon by the time they arrived, and Rosie had half fallen asleep on the ride home, reaching out of hold Alana's arm as she rested.

"Come one sleeping beauty," Alana said as she got out and walked around to Rosie's door. Opening it, Alana took off Rosie's seat belt and helped her out of the car before they made their way inside. Ignoring the maids who worked silently as Alana and Rosie walked through the house, they made their way to Rosie's bedroom and locked the door behind them.

"Finally!" Rosie said, falling onto her bed and closing her eyes.

"You need a shower, little one, Mommy can't have you going to bed all dirty from the day,"

Alana said, going into the bathroom and beginning to run Rosie a bath. Rosie got up and slowly made her way to the bathroom sitting on the edge of the bath as Alana undressed her.

"I thought you were a big girl little one, looks like you are a sweet baby when you are sleepy," Alana said, stroking Rosie's cheeks with her thumbs. Rosie just nodded her head while looking up at Alana, raising her arms as Alana lifted her into the bath.

"Oh bubbles, Mommy, that's nice," Rosie said, splashing in the bath happily.

"I'm really happy to be here with you, baby girl," Alana said, making Rosie smile a toothy grin and swim over to where Alana was sitting. She placed her head on Alana's lap, wetting her jeans slightly.

"I'm glad as well Mommy, I missed you, I need you," Rosie said lovingly before going back to splashing in the tub.

Alana watched Rosie until the water turned cold and got her out, drying her off and making her giggle as her toes where dried.

"Mommy," Rosie said as she balanced on one foot. Alana took her back into her room and sat Rosie down on the ottoman at the end of her bed.

"I did some shopping, Mommy," Rosie said, pointing to the cupboard. Alana walked over to see that Rosie had a collection of adult onesies and diapers, pacifiers and baby bottles.

"My my haven't you been busy baby girl," Alana said, running her fingers over the collection of diapers that Rosie had neatly stacked in her cupboard. Selecting the purple stripe one and a grey onesie Alana made her way back over to Rosie, who looked nervous and excited at the same time.

"Are you going to lay down for Mommy?" Alana asked Rosie, who was already resting on her elbows. Alana reached for the baby powder that Rosie passed her and rubbed it over Rosie's body, bending down to kiss the tip of her nose.

"Thank you for letting me be your Mommy

baby girl," Alana said to Rosie, who giggled and reached for her toes, getting gentle spanks on her thighs from Alana, who pushed her legs back down.

"Keep your leggies down for Mommy little one," Alana said, sticking the tabs of the diaper down and running her hands over the top of Rosie's diapered bottom as Rosie turned over and tried to tuck herself into bed.

"Not just yet little cuteness," Alana said, grabbing Rosie by the ankle and pulling her back so she could dress her in the onesie.

"You have to put your jammies on, sweetheart," Alana said, dressing Rosie.

"And teethies," Alana laughed as Rosie pouted before getting a warning look from Alana.

"You haven't been punished by mommy yet, don't let it be tonight, little one," Alana said, walking Rosie to the bathroom again.

"Mommy, am I done now?" Rosie begged turning the light off to the bathroom after she had cleaned her teeth for 3 minutes and not a second longer and looking at Alana pleadingly.

"Yes, little one, it's bedtime," Alana laughed, taking Rosie's hand and pulling back her bedsheets.

"Mommy, are you coming in?" Rosie asked Alana, who took off her jacket.

"Mommy hasn't had a shower yet little one, can you stay up for five more minutes?" Alana asked, kicking off her boots and unzipping her jeans, revealing her red lace thong. Rosie smiled and nodded, enjoying the look of Alana's body and wanting it in bed with her.

Alana came back 20minutes later with just a towel around her waist, smiling at Rosie, who was fast asleep. Alana threw the dry towel on the floor before climbing into bed with Rosie, who opened her eyes and snuggled into Alana's arms, readjusting her position several times before Alana spoke to her.

"Shh baby girl Mommy is here," Alana said while holding Rosie and patting her back. Rosie murmured something Alana couldn't understand before she took a deep breath and fell back into her sleep. Alana stayed awake. Thinking about how close she had been to losing Rosie forever and held her tighter as she remembered how Rosie had looked at her with venom in her eyes earlier in the day. *That was close*, Alana thought, stroking Rosie's hair out of her face and sighing in relief as she closed her eyes and went to sleep.

Alana and Rosie spent the next day locked up in Rosie's room, not wanting to burst the bubble they had finally been able to create. With the wall-length windows opened to the outdoor courtyard, Rosie had enjoyed a day spent rolling around in bed, relaxing in Alana's arms, and playing in her little space.

"Baby, do you think we should leave the house today?" Alana asked as she got dressed, coming out from having a shower. Rosie shook her head at which Alana just smirked and went to her cupboard to pick out what she wanted to dress her in.

"Well that's alright, we are going to go out anyway," Alana replied, taking Rosie by the hand and leading her to the bed.

"No, Mommy," Rosie said, squirming on her back, not wanting to be undressed. Alana stopped and thought for a moment before unbuckling the belt she had just secured to her hips. Slowly taking it off, she clapped the buckle into her hand before doubling the leather over.

"No, Mommy?" Alana questioned, jumping onto the bed to straddle Rosie, who tried to push her off. Alana stayed firmly positioned on top of Rosie before lifting off her enough to turn her over and pin her down with her leg.

"Baby girl, do not say no to Mommy," Alana said calmly before striking Rosie on her diapered bottom. Rosie stopped resisting her and lay still, pouting and trying to fight back the tears. Knowing that Rosie's limits were easily reached, Alana let her up and turned her back to face her. She put her hands on either side of Rosie's cheeks and looked at her baby girl, lovingly.

"Don't say no to Mommy, do you understand me?" Alana said gently, opening her arms and holding onto Rosie tightly. Rosie buried her head in Alana's ample cleavage and nodded her head.

"Use your words baby girl, Mommy wants to hear it," Alana said, rocking her back and forth.

"Yes, Mommy," Rosie said quietly, bringing her thumb up to suck only for it to be taken out of her mouth and replaced with a paci.

"Let Mommy dress you in something else, baby," Alana said, going back to dressing a far more compliant Rosie. Alana chose a tight-fitting pull-up, a pair of high waisted jeans and a sleeveless button-down that gaped at the neck.

"Are you helping Mommy put on your sockies, baby girl?" Alana asked as Rosie nodded and fiddled with one of her socks before Alana slid on heeled beige boots and finished the look with a lightweight trench coat.

"Very cute," Alana said as she pushed a black pacifier in Rosie's mouth and watched her in her little space while she got dressed.

"Where are we going, Mommy?" Rosie asked as Alana put her hair up in a messy ponytail and checked her phone.

"Somewhere I think you'll like little one, come on," Alana said, holding out her hand to Rosie, who excitedly jumped down from her bed and ran to hold Alana's hand.

Chapter 11

"Mommy, can you tell me now?" Rosie whispered into Alana's ear as they sat in the back of the town car that was driving them to the undisclosed location. Alana had seen the night before that there was a private party invite from one of her friends in an email and just knew that Rosie would love to go. The private parties of celebrities, Alana had learned were more scandalous than anything the tabloids could ever report, and this one was set to be the biggest event of the year.

"No sweetie," Alana said, pulling Rosie closer to her and rubbing her hand over the front of Rosie's pussy, her jeans muffling the crinkly sound of her pull up.

"Such a sweet baby girl," Alana said almost to herself, getting lost in the feeling of protective love that flowed through her instantly.

"I love you, Rosie," Alana said abruptly, the words escaping before she could stop them, holding her breath as she heard what she had just said.

"I know Mommy," Rosie said, repositioning herself against Alana, who was now cradling Rosie in her arms. The car stopped, and Alana got out slowly, taking in the lavish gardens of the property they were to spend the next couple of days. Alana had packed Rosie's bikini and a few other things she thought they might need in an over-night bag. She knew that these parties tended to last far longer than an evening. Rosie held Alana's hand as they walked up the path, hiding behind Alana when they waited at the front door.

"Is this the part where you sell me to the red light district?" Rosie said fearfully. Alana looked down and was amused by Rosie's imagination.

"No, sweetheart, we are going to a party," Alana replied, smiling as she saw Rosie's face light up.

"Oh cool," Rosie said, adopting her usual confident manner and reaching out to knock on the door again. Banging loudly, Rosie impatiently stamped her foot but jumped as the door swung open.

"Hey cutie," Said a woman that Rosie knew instantly. Speechless, Rosie just grabbed on Alana's arm and turned, walking back down the steps of the mansions and onto the gravel driveway.

"What the fuck, Alana?" Rosie yelled once she saw the door of the house shut. Alana rolled her eyes, annoyed Rosie was freaking out.

"What?" Alana replied. She had thought that Rosie would have liked to blow off some steam and was unsure of why Rosie was acting this way.

"Do you know who she is?!" Rosie squealed to Alana's amusement.

"Yes. And?" Alana asked, not caring about who the IT girl was who had opened the door.

"She's just a naughty baby like you, darling. Didn't you know?" Alana said, making Rosie pout.

"I'm not naughty," she said, folding her arms against her chest and stepping side to side, unsure of how to process what she had just seen. The woman had been wearing a tight black t-shirt, white diaper, and thigh-high rainbow socks. Her hair was pulled up into two messy pigtails, and the silver chained collar that hung around her neck had made Rosie wonder how her fragile-looking body could hold such an object.

"You said it was a party!" Rosie said, shaking her head, trying to somehow make sense of this.

"It is, it's a party for Mommies and babies. Come on, you're silly," Alana said as Rosie sat down on the gravel.

"I don't wanna go, Mommy," Rosie said, looking up at Alana with a serious face that made Alana second guess if she was too mean making Rosie go.

"Well, what shall we do instead baby girl?" Alana said, coming to sit down next to Rosie, who leaned over and rested her head on Alana's shoulder.

"Could we just go home, please, Mommy?" Rosie said softly, taking Alana's hand and looking up at her with puppy dog eyes. Alana sighed and knew why Rosie didn't want to go in. Her whole world would end if the media got a hold of this information. The information that she was just a baby girl who needed Mommy to look after her. Alana stood up and held out her hand to Rosie, who took it eagerly and cuddled into Alana as they walked to where their car was.

"Thank you, Mommy," Rosie whispered as Alana buckled her into the car, tenderly reaching up and playing with Alana's hair making Alana smile at her lovingly.

"It's OK, baby girl; Mommy is going to look after you always. I'm excited to see what games we play when we get home though little one. I have big plans for you tonight. And to get you ready, spread your legs for me," Alana instructed, waiting for Rosie to follow her request. Rosie obediently parted her thighs and gasped when Alana reached into her pull up and placed a vibrating egg against her clit just as their driver turned around the corner.

"Keep quiet little one, nobody wants to hear your moans," Alana said before kissing the top of Rosie's forehead. Alana walked around to the other side of the car and got in, holding Rosie's hand and enjoying her squirming and pressing her head against the back of the chair as the car drove over bumps and holes on the road, making her clit ache and her pussy wet.

"Mommy, please," Rosie said the minute the door was shut behind them, making Alana laugh and rub Rosie over her pull up only adding to her frustration.

"Are you a horny little girl? Do you need Mommy to fuck you, baby?" Alana teased as she went to the bedroom, followed by Rosie, who willingly let Alana push her onto the bed.

"Let me see baby," Alana said, unzipping Rosie's jeans and reaching into her pull up only to push the vibrating egg into her pussy roughly.

"You'll take it one way or the other baby girl, Mommy is going to play rough with you tonight," Alana said going to the wooden chest they kept their sex toys in and took out a long black leather whip and a bit gag. Alana gently secured the gag behind Rosie's head, enjoying how she had to stretch her mouth wide to hold it.

"Such a pretty little slut," Alana said, taking off Rosie's shirt and biting into her, making her wriggle, only stopping when Alana placed her hand on her neck and squeezed.

"No, don't move little one," Alana said, bringing her whip down on Rosie's tummy, making her bite down on the gag, Alana enjoying her muffled screams. Alana marked her until Rosie was only wincing with each strike and placing the whip down, she took Rosie's pull up off. She took out the vibrator only to quickly replace it with her strap-on. She flipped Rosie and bucked her hips as she slapped her ass, making Rosie ride her deeply, Rosie's hands coming to rest on Alana's tits as she was fucked.

"Mommy wants to fuck you like I've paid you baby girl. Are you going to let Mommy have everything I want tonight?" Alana said to Rosie, who just nodded her head and matched Alana's thrusts.

"You'll take everything Mommy gives you baby girl, I told you I was going to enjoy you tonight darling," Alana said calmly as Rosie was fucked raw, her cries only encouraging Alana. As Rosie closed her eyes, Alana slowed her onslaught and took out the gag only to replace it with her cum covered strap.

"Suck you pussy juices clean off baby girl, such a dirty little girl, you'll say yes to anything won't you baby," Alana said, pushing her strap down Rosie's gaging throat. Suddenly taking it out of her mouth and releasing the firm grip she had on Rosie's head.

"I'm not finished with you yet, sweetheart," Alana loving whispered in Rosie's ear as she kissed her neck and ran her finger-tips over Rosie's still warm tummy, the marks of Alana's whip clear and red on her Irish white skin. Alana walked out of the room, leaving Rosie to lay spent on her bed as she thought about how she had come so far, now being able to love a woman. *I know that there are other people out there that could give me something similar, maybe better in some instances even. But I want what she can give me. I can be little with her one minute and completely dominant in the next, and she can keep up. I'm free with her, it's nice. I like that she likes to control everything but that she listens to me and bends where I need and want her too. I like that I hate everyone but her, they are just so fucking boring and pointless.* Rosie's thoughts were interrupted by the huge object Alana had come back into the room with. A giant brown teddy bear with a long thick strap-on firmly attached from the inside made Rosie's mouth gaped open.

"Good, keep that pretty mouth open, baby girl, you're going to play with teddy tonight," Alana said, putting the teddy's cock into her mouth, forcing it down her throat.

"Suck," Alana said, slapping Rosie's face several times and pinching her nose as Rosie gaged and panted as her mouth was filled.

"Pretty little slut," Alana said affectionately watching Rosie service the teddy. Alana placed the bear in the middle of the bed and grabbed Rosie by a fistful of hair.

"Do you know how Mommy wants to watch you play tonight, little girl?" Alana said with an evil laugh in her voice. Rosie nodded her head painfully as her hair pulled with every motion.

"Use your big girl words, baby," Alana said, loosening her grip but spanking Rosie's ass.

"You want me to ride teddy?" Rosie questioned, getting a nod of approval from Alana, who let her go and took a step back.

"Begin," Alana commanded, getting wet as she saw Rosie position herself over the teddy's cock. Impatient of Rosie's hesitation, Alana walked back over to the bed and pushed Rosie down by the shoulders, making her pussy full of the teddy's cock. Alana knew that the toy was stretching her by the sudden gasp of air the filled Rosie's lungs as the teddy was slammed into her. However, Alana enjoyed the grinding of Rosie's hips that followed, taking her whip and striking Rosie's ass several times.

"Fuck your teddy baby girl," Alana said as she began whipping Rosie again. Rosie lifted her hips off the cock to drop them down again, panting as she bounced on her teddy fuck buddy.

"Fuck, this is hotter than I had thought it would be," Alana said breathlessly, bending Rosie over the bear and pinning her down, making her feel the cock deeper inside of her.

"Mommy," Rosie said in the exhausted voice Alana had been waiting to hear.

"Just a little longer, baby girl, you're not done just yet," Alana said, coming behind her and guiding her lubed slim strap-on into Rosie's ass, making her shake her hips. Alana held them firmly in place as she pushed into Rosie, who continued to fuck her teddy until she lay spent over the large soft toy as Alana fucked her ass until she was satisfied Rosie would need a full day to recover.

"Cute little girl, I love it how you are so good for me," Alana said, slowly sliding out of Rosie and pulling her limp body from the teddy who still had it's cock filling her pussy. Alana carried Rosie to the floor and rubbed cream over her red marks and wrapped her in her favorite snuggly blanket.

"Come to Mommy, little one, let me give you all the cuddles," Alana said, picking up Rosie's bunny and smiling down at it.

"Bunny wants to give you kisses," Alana said as she lay down next to Rosie, playfully bopping Rosie on the nose with the toy.

"Mommy," Rosie said, exhaustion in her voice. Alana wrapped her arms around Rosie and squeezed her, holding her lovingly into the night.

Chapter 12

"What time is that interview you've got tonight, sweetheart?" Alana said, rolling over in bed and pulling Rosie to her. Rosie flinched, Alana had put her through a particularly painful session the night before, and she was still feeling it this morning.

"I don't even want to think about it, Mommy. They are going to want to talk about the movie and ask me if I'm dating someone and why I've been hiding on social media. I wish I could go up there and say I'm retiring," Rosie said, playing with Alana's breasts as she cuddled on top of her. Alana ran her fingers through Rosie's somehow perfect bed hair and marveled at how stunning her baby girl was.

"Oh, Mommy's sweet girl wants to call it quits?" Alana teased, making Rosie roll her eyes.

"Yes," Rosie said confidently, causing Alana

to laugh. Alana moved up the bed and sat up, keeping Rosie on her lap as she pat her bottom gently.

"You can say whatever the fuck you want, sweetheart," Alana said, wishing she had a cigarette to smoke. It was these types of moments where she realized just how much she used to smoke after giving it up when Rosie started to have Asthma flare-ups the longer they stayed together. Quitting had caused Alana to gain a couple of pounds, which had delighted Rosie to have something more to snuggle into and bigger tits for her to suck and play with.

"Well, now that I have your permission," Rosie laughed, rolling off Alana and heading to the bathroom. Alana watched as she walked away. The marks on her back still present, and the bruise on her neck beginning to show made Alana smile to herself.

Rosie was whisked away in the afternoon by her people, who picked her up three hours before the interview was scheduled. Rosie had kept them waiting for an extra half-hour as she let Alana change her back into a big girl after their morning of playing. Alana had decided she would stay in, opting for eating snacks and swimming in the pool while she waited for her sweet baby to return. She had moved into Rosie's mansion much to her amusement. She had thought it would be the other way around, but when Rosie pointed out that she was, in fact, a millionaire and that living in her home would make more sense because it was bigger and had more fun things to do than Alana's, Alana didn't feel like disputing the facts. They had been living here for almost five months, and in that time Alana liked that Rosie happily gave her full control over the domain. Alana had stayed working, taking on clients that had no idea of her relationship with the starlet but seeming always to have something to say about her. If Alana was honest, it was beginning to wear her thin. Having these people speak about her baby girl so negatively all the while being obsessed with her every move made Alana want to reveal the relationship every time.

Alana got out of the pool and dried off on the sunbed before turning on the TV to watch the interview. The media had hyped it with such intensity because it was going to go live and completely unedited.

Alana held her breath as she saw her baby girl walk onto the interviewing platform as she entered, stopping to wave to people and strike a few playful poses.

"Mommy's sweet baby," Alana said out loud as she sat down in the living room and crossed her legs on the sofa.

"So tonight we have the one and only Rosie Smith with us for her exclusive, reveal all interview about her debut film, juicy set secrets, and an apparent mystery lover," the female presenter began, gaining a predictable response of applause from the audience.

"Rosie, your latest gig, if you like, is that blockbusting movie, *Nowhere South*. Tell us, how did you land the role?" The interviewer asked as Rosie nodded her head. Alana liked watching her body language, she knew Rosie didn't want to be there, she always bit both lips when she was trying to hurry up a lecture Alana was giving her and as Alana saw both her lips being bitten she laughed.

"Well, it's a funny story. I went to a party a few months ago, and by went I really mean, I walked up to the front door and then decided I'd rather stay at home with a special someone," Rosie said pausing and looking directly into the camera as Alana choked on the chips she was eating at the statement Rosie had just made. It hadn't only caused Alana to be surprised; the audience became hysterical with cheers, gasps, and applause.

"Then a few weeks after that, the host of the party called me up asking if I'd audition for the role of Jaz, I read the script and got the part," Rosie continued with a victorious smirk. The interviewer looked excited at where the interview was going yet stepped carefully as to gain the response she wanted.

"That is fantastic. Tell us more about this mystery, man," she said, making Rosie smirk at her.

"I never said it was a man," Rosie replied quickly, making the audience became hysterical all over again. Meanwhile, Alana was glued to the TV, wondering how far she was going to go with all of this.

"I'm in a relationship with an older woman, I have been for almost a year," Rosie said triumphantly as she looked at the speechless interviewer who was clearing trying to think what questions she could ask next. Rosie waited until the applause died down before she spoke again.

"Is that what you all wanted? To leach onto my private life and suck me dry of insight and information?" Rosie began to say, a different tone falling over the audience.

"Well, is it?" Rosie prompted. Looking toward the interviewer, she began to speak candidly.

"You see, this is the thing about people

knowing about your existence, I don't think you could even call it fame, it's just knowledge of you. They want to unpack everything you have, your life, your soul; it's almost like a drug for you people. You invade every part of my life, and it is never enough. You all have opinions about me, and yet, you don't know anything about me, you only know what has either been shared as my social mask, my branding or what has been stolen from me. And the sad part about this is that it's not just me. You people do this to everyone you claim to love. It's not loving, it's an obsession, I'm the drug dealer to your addiction, and I came on today to let you know that I am not going to be supplying you anymore. From this December, I will be retiring. I deserve peace; I deserve a life that uplifts me, my relationship deserves it, and so does my Mommy," Rosie said before smiling directly at Alana who was in tears of joy as she watched Rosie stand, wave to the audience who were speechless and disappeared off the screen. Alana ran to the kitchen bench and grabbed her phone, frantically dialing Rosie's number.

"Hey, Mommy," Rosie said, sounding like she had just offloaded the weight of the world.

"My sweet baby, come home to Mommy," Alana said lovingly, causing Rosie to giggle.

"I'm already in the car," Rosie replied before hanging up, placing her phone down, closing her eyes and breathing for the first time in what felt like years.

I wandered out onto the beach, the soft, warm sand between my toes as I watched the morning rays rise over the ocean. When I think about all of the women I had used to curb the emptiness in my heart, it makes me laugh. It's not as though the world stopped turning, or my blood was rushed with lust. It was a whisper in the night, a daring, a chance at something that was never meant to be tasted. Innocence is sexy, weakness is alluring, and nothing says take me like the eyes of a watcher, or was it just me. Rosebud lips parting with forced consent, it must have been fun. How many more times do you need to be honored and held in the highest regard before you understand that you are magnificent?

You built an empire on every other brick they threw at you, you don't need to use this one as a cornerstone. You don't need to be so hard on yourself when all you have ever done is rise. Has there been anything you have started and not finished with such excellence that people think you are lucky? Have you ever backed down from a challenge? Haven't you fought every evil that dared stand against you? Please don't tell me that you've forgotten who you truly are, what I fucking made you?! I hadn't thought you'd be so easily confused. You see it, don't you when you look in the mirror? You see who you truly are. You were never weak, you were never scared, and you were certainly never meant to politely let them take from you for fun my darling. And yet here we are, going over the same thing we always do, aren't you sick of it? I know it makes your blood boil, I know it makes your soul ache, I know it makes you bare your teeth, wanting to fight. It's fucking meant to. It's meant to drive you; it's meant to pound your heart and emanate protection and strength. You were never meant to be anything but an amazing light. You did it yesterday, didn't you? You did it last week, you do it every fucking day for them, and you can't figure out how to do it for yourself? What the hell are you waiting for? Is it too much? Do you burn too brightly for even you to handle? Is that why you yield to them? Why you kneel? Did you get told that your confidence was too offensive one time too many and start to give a fuck what those reptilian fuck dolls had to say? How dare you forget. How dare you try and challenge how I made you.

Get very fucking comfortable with your light, my darling; I'm not taking it away, the world needs you far too much for that. You need it far too much for that. Don't you know that when you let your soul roar, it is heard for miles and felt over the seas? Don't you understand that I gave you this gift for a reason? There is no one else, so stop asking for the baton to be passed, it is yours, and you will rise with *the weight of responsibility resting on your shoulders like the solider that you are. Don't be afraid of it. Have I not been here with you the whole time?*

Rosie closed her laptop lid as she heard Alana's footsteps behind her coming from their back steps and out onto the sand.

"What are you doing, baby girl?" Alana asked, spreading her legs and sitting behind Rosie, pulling her back slightly and into her embrace.

"I'm just writing, Mommy," Rosie replied as she showed Alana her work. Alana took the time to read it, stopping and thinking after the page had been read twice.

"This very deep baby girl, are you talking to yourself?" Alana asked, bending around to look Rosie in the eye. The waves of the cold ocean crashed down, and crabs ran across the white sand. Rosie watched them dig holes to hide from the morning sun before she spoke again.

"Yeah, I was. I was talking to myself like if the older me could talk to me now. I use to be so worried about what or who was talking about me, how they acted, or reacted with the things I did. It was the game I was playing, but what I hadn't realized was that it was hurting me. Now speaking my truth was killing me, having people constantly invading my spaces just became way too much and honestly, if it hadn't had been for this last year, I don't even want to know what my life would have turned out like," Rosie said resting her head on Alana's shoulder. Alana stroked her hair and held her tight, she thought back on her life over the past year and agreed, she didn't want to think about how different it would have been without Rosie either.

"So, you like being my sweet girl then?" Alana said, taking the laptop away from her and placing it down next to where they were sitting. Rosie nodded, and Alana smiled as she took out a pacifier from her pocket and gently placed it in Rosie's mouth. Rosie looked at Alana, her eyes telling Alana all she needed to know.

"Good, because I am not interested in

having our life any other way," Alana said, picking Rosie up and taking her back inside.

Who is Tina Moore?

Tina Moore has enjoyed the lifestyle of a Mommy Domme for several years. She began exploring kink and BDSM in her youth and found her love of being a strict Mommy Domme in early 2000. Tina Moore is now an author of many MDLG and ABDL themed novels.

Having enjoyed many years in the kink community, Tina Moore combines these experiences with the sweet and naughty things her baby girl does to bring you tantalizing and salacious stories.

Follow her on:

Author Page on Amazon

Instagram @tinamoore.kdp